Ferret Fun

By **Karen Rostoker-Gruber**

Illustrated by **Paul Rátz de Tagyos**

Marshall Cavendish Children

Marshall Cavendish Corporation, 99 White Plains Road, Tarrytown, NY 10591
www.marshallcavendish.us/kids

Library of Congress Cataloging-in-Publication Data
Rostoker-Gruber, Karen.
Ferret fun / by Karen Rostoker-Gruber ; illustrated by Paul Ratz de
Tagyos.—1st ed.
p. cm.
Summary: Two nervous pet ferrets named Fudge and Einstein try to convince
a visiting cat that they are not mouth-watering rats.
ISBN 978-0-7614-5817-3
[1. Ferrets as pets—Fiction. 2. Pets—Fiction. 3. Cats—Fiction.] I. Ratz
de Tagyos, Paul, ill. II. Title.
PZ7.R72375Fe 2011
[E]—dc22
2010021301

The illustrations are rendered in marker and ink.
Book design by Anahid Hamparian
Editor: Margery Cuyler

Printed in Malaysia [T]   First edition   1 3 5 6 4 2

Marshall Cavendish
Children

For my ferret, Bandit, and to Dr. David Costlow, DVM, and Norma Ellis, who always take care of Bandit when we are away. Also a very special thanks to Sammy, Dr. Costlow's cat, who became Bandit's playmate during an overnight stay.

— K.R-G.

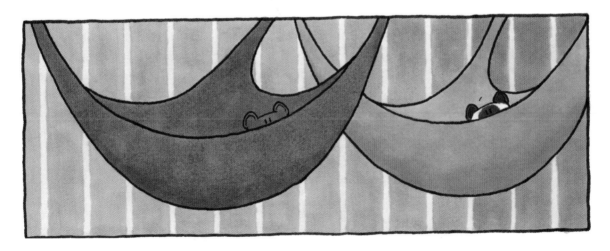

To K.R-G., whose advocacy on my behalf made my participation in this book possible. And to Anna . . . just 'cause.

— P.R.D.T.

Fudge and Einstein were taking a nap when Andrea, their owner, came into the room. They poked their heads out of their hammocks.

Fudge . . . Einstein. I want you to meet a friend of mine.

Marvel is staying with us while her owner is away.

I hope this friend brought raisins.

I love raisins.

Andrea set Marvel down on the rug.

WHAT ARE YOU TWO? YOU'RE NOT CATS. I KNOW CATS. YOU'RE NOT DOGS. I KNOW DOGS. ARE YOU RATS?

I LOVE TASTY— I MEAN—I LOVE RATS.

Uh . . . we're ferrets.

Marvel's eyes narrowed into angry, slanted slits.

That's no friend.

No kidding.

Marvel lay down next to the cage and closed her eyes.

I'll be back in a minute.

As soon as Andrea left, Marvel opened her eyes and stretched.

Marvel walked in front of the ferret cage.

I'VE OPENED A FEW CAGES IN MY DAY.

Both ferrets dove into their hammocks.

We're ferret flambé fur sure!

Marvel pawed at the latch of the ferret cage.

Nothing.

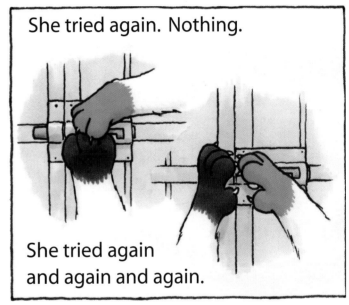

She tried again. Nothing.

She tried again and again and again.

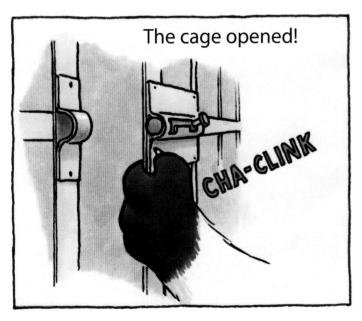

The cage opened!

CHA-CLINK

Marvel reached her paw

into the cage and ...

…just then, Andrea came back.

Marvel quickly backed away and scampered to her sleeping spot.

Marvel, it's time for your milk.

Andrea picked up Marvel.

We've got to do something or we're ferret fritters fur-ever!

What can we do?

We could hide.

She'll find us.

We could ignore her.

She'll bug us more.

We could run away.

Then who would feed us raisins?

It's no use. We're doomed.

Wait! I've got it. Let's hide in the closet. If that feisty feline finds us, we'll stand up to her. There's two of us and only one of her.

Yeah. She'll never expect that.

It will scare the hair balls out of her!

Einstein went out the cage door and raced to the closet.

Fudge ran after him.

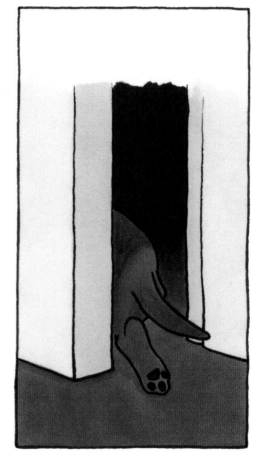

After a while, Marvel walked back into the room.

WHERE 'D YOU GO, YOU LITTLE RATS?

AH-HA! I CAN SMELL YOU IN THAT CLOSET.

RAT (ferret)

YOU KNOW I CAN'T EAT, I MEAN "PLAY" WITH YOU IF YOU'RE HIDING.

Marvel dove into the closet.

Fudge and Einstein puffed out their fur,
arched their backs, bared their sharp teeth,
and hissed.

We're NOT rats!

And we've had enough NOW

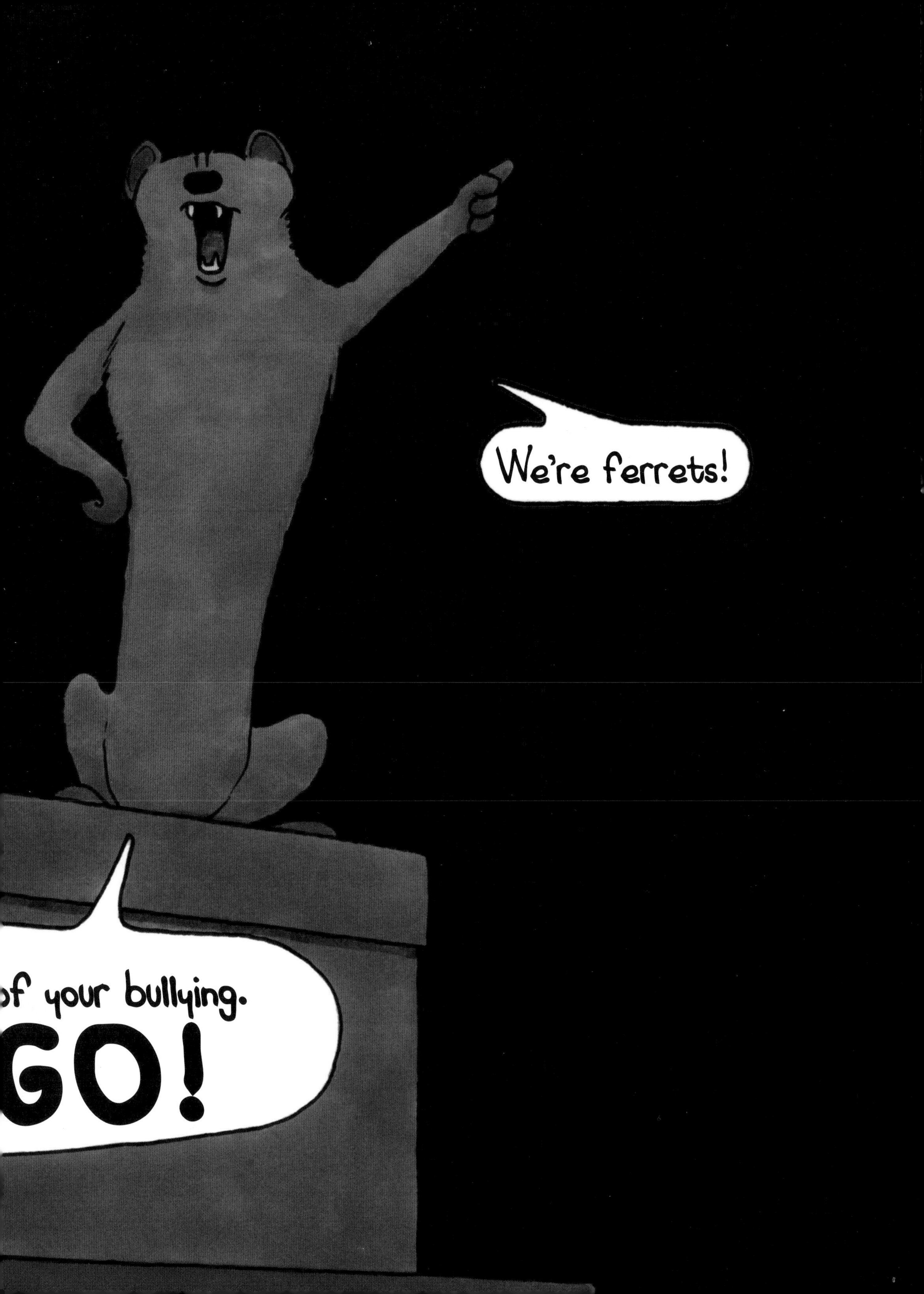
We're ferrets!
of your bullying.
GO!

Then they lunged toward Marvel.
Boxes upon boxes upon boxes tumbled to the floor.

A box hit Marvel on the head.

ME-OWWWCH!

She dashed out of the closet, through the ferret room, and into the hall.

Fudge and Einstein did their happy dance.

They ran back to their cage and curled up in their hammocks.

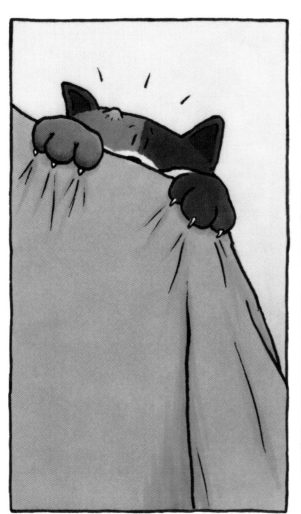

Andrea and Marvel came back into the room.

Marvel, it was just some boxes crashing down.

Marvel's fur relaxed—a bit.
Andrea pulled Marvel's claws
from her shirt.

Marvel, you stay here while I go make dinner.

They nudged a raisin container toward Marvel.

Marvel looked at the raisin container. Then she looked at Fudge and Einstein. Their fur wasn't puffed up, their backs weren't arched, and they weren't baring their sharp teeth or hissing. They looked…friendly.

Marvel opened the container and watched Fudge and Einstein eat and eat and eat.

Fudge pushed some raisins over to Marvel.

Do you want some?

Marvel wasn't sure.